ROYDEN POOLE'S

FIELD GUIDE

TO THE 25TH HOUR

Also from

BROKEN EYE BOOKS

The Hole Behind Midnight, by Clinton J. Boomer
Crooked, by Richard Pett
Scourge of the Realm, by Erik Scott de Bie
By Faerie Light, edited by Scott Gable & C. Dombrowski
Ghost in the Cogs, edited by Scott Gable & C. Dombrowski
Tomorrow's Cthulhu, edited by Scott Gable & C. Dombrowski

COMING SOON
Izanami's Choice, by Adam Heine

www.brokeneyebooks.com
Blowing minds, one book at a time. Broken Eye Books publishes the weird
side of science fiction, fantasy, and horror. We love it all, and the blurrier the
boundaries, the better.

ROYDEN POOLE'S
FIELD
GUIDE
TO THE 25TH HOUR

woo,
mother-fucker

Clinton J. Boomer

CLINTON J. BOOMER

ROYDEN POOLE'S FIELD GUIDE TO THE 25TH HOUR
Published by
Broken Eye Books
www.brokeneyebooks.com

Copyright © 2016 Broken Eye Books and Clinton J. Boomer
Cover design by Matt Youngmark
Interior design by Scott Gable
Editing by Scott Gable, C. Dombrowski,
and Dora Wang

ISBN-10: 1-940372-19-4
ISBN-13: 978-1-940372-19-8

Table of Contents

Royden Poole's Field Guide to the 25th Hour
is a collection of stories written by Clinton J. Boomer.
It uses the same characters and is set in the same world
established in his novel *The Hole Behind Midnight*.

Occasionally, during my day-to-day life
—especially while working at the bar—
I'll receive insanely detailed monologues, musings,
manifestos, and memoirs from one of my characters.
These arrive unbidden in the back of my skull,
and all I can do is transcribe them.

These "floating chapters" within the 25th Hour
represent such instances.

Please, enjoy responsibly.

As always, for my mom
(despite, as always, her very specific request
that I not dedicate this to her).

—Clinton J. Boomer

On Airports

Clinton J. Boomer

Cleon and I stood there, calmly waiting in line for the TSA people to get around to sticking their fingers in our ears and mouths. We blankly watched a three-hundred-pound high school dropout in an ill-fitting, mustard-stained uniform take a seventy-year-old woman's nail clippers from her and throw them away.

My boarding pass and passport were crumpled and sweat-slick in my hand.

Somewhere, my belt and my shoes were sitting on a rubber conveyor belt, being irradiated.

I had my lighter hidden in my underwear.

I had my cigarettes tucked between my butt cheeks.

I needed a smoke so bad, I could taste it.

I remained calm.

I hate airports.

I'm not the only one, I'm sure, but I just wanted to make it known at this point to you, the reader, that I'm not stupid enough to have some sort of farcical opinion about how nice an airport can be. Oh, how it shimmers and sparkles in the early winter's light, like a needle hanging from the pale arm of an overdosed heroin addict or some other such bullshit.

It would be pretty embarrassing for both of us—you and me alike—to discover that I'm actually an old softie under all my gritty posturing and confrontational self-loathing and angry bitterness.

I fucking *hate* airports.

I also hate Christmas, in case you happened to be wondering.

Now, to be totally clear on this, there are many people who like to talk about how nice airports are. Especially around Christmas.

And I suppose it is a lovely sentiment, after all, to find joy in something as soulless and banal and industrial-grade, vacuum-sealed, single-serving shitbrick frustrating-dull as an airport. Honestly, there's a whole monologue from the movie *Love Actually* where Hugh Grant goes on and on about how the fucking arrivals gate at Heathrow Airport can be seen as some sort of ever-enduring symbol of human goodness and love.

Especially at Christmas.

Which must be nice for Hugh Grant.

The thing is, I hate people. Just, you know, in general. Stupid people, mostly, but even smart people get on my nerves.

It's not just because I'm some eternal outsider, either: I actually met another third-generation, Indian-American midget with a drinking problem and a master's-level background in history, and the two of us loathed each other instantly.

I hate being around people, and I hate dealing with people, and I hate it when things as simple as my complexion and my temper and my propensity for one-liners make me the most likely candidate for a quick strip search.

The problem is, I think, that the airport isn't the real world.

No, it's somehow *worse*.

In the real world, at least, it's considered somewhat rude to stare at dark-skinned dudes my size and secretly wonder if I'm the shortest member of Al-Qaeda. Like, maybe, I'm their mascot or something.

But not at the airport.

Here, it's standard operating procedure.

And the food is terrible. And the lighting sucks. And it's cold. And everyone is rude, so my rudeness doesn't even stand out until I get security called on me. And the hurry-up-and-wait bullshit and the no-smoking rules and the fact that your baggage might get stolen or blown up or lost, well . . . that all just makes it hell on earth.

Plus, if there's one place in the world where you just *cannot* simply slide sideways into the Nether Hour, it's the airport. Because somebody is watching fucking everything. Every goddamn, horrible, garishly lit inch of the place.

That person watching you might be incompetent, underpaid, angry, and stupid, but someone is watching.

No thin spots or slippy holes around here.

Yet somehow, when you're stuck in the nether and need to get out, the airport is simply never there for you. Just a big, empty field full of broken linoleum tile and torn-up fencing, and you can kind of hear the roaring of far-off jet engines, and there's a lot of litter and flashing lights in the sky as the edges of reality get blurry—but you cannot, for the life of you, get home to the Real.

I hate it.

Also, fuck you for judging me for having seen *Love Actually*. It used to be one of Tama's favorites, and the part where the British kid, Colin, goes to Wisconsin is fucking hilarious.

And anything with Bill Nighy is amazing, especially with his advice about buying drugs.

That still cracks me up.

Anyway, we stood there and watched the poor old woman's shoes get taken away from her, and her husband got mad, and security got called, and I'm pretty sure they missed their flight.

I frowned.

Cleon nudged me on the shoulder and hissed. "Stop scowling."

"I'm not scowling. I'm frowning—there's a difference."

He said nothing.

"I'm not going to get tased again. I swear."

He said nothing.

"I'm not going to yell 'bomb,' either."

He glared at me—as did several other passengers.

I looked around. "Fuck all you people. So, Cleon, who is this paranoid asshole we're supposed to be meeting, again?"

Cleon rolled his eyes. "He was the longshot guy I was talking about, who I wasn't sure if I could get ahold of or not. He knows how we can contact the Sultans of Swing—they used to do courier and transportation security work for him."

This time, I rolled my eyes. "I know that. But who is he?"

Cleon shrugged. "Nobody really important. The Third Earl of Quashquema."

"Never heard of it."

"Yeah, I figured."

I scratched my ass and thought for a minute. "So why is he so paranoid that we have to be woken up at eleven in the morning by a FedEx guy with a box containing only the instructions to buy tickets on a noon flight that we don't even want to take?"

"Three things. First, I wasn't asleep, lazy ass. Second, this guy is dumb or ill-informed or both, so he thinks our powers are weakest at noon. And third, it's so we have to go through security to meet him and can't bring . . . *weapons*. The last-minute, hop-to-it bullshit is just so we can't prep to have a contingency plan in place."

"What, like a sniper on the tarmac?"

Cleon glared at me and grinned and waved casually at several of the people whose attention I'd inadvertently caught. "Yes, exactly like that."

"Fine. So why the fuck is he so paranoid? You'd think this guy was the pope."

Cleon shrugged again. "Well, he's also technically an heir in line to the Forgotten Throne of Carthage."

That got my attention. "What, seriously? *Carthage*? I thought those mad Roman-killing bastards were power players out of Tunisia."

Cleon sighed and rolled his eyes even harder. "Not the Phoenician one, dummy. The one in Hancock County."

I blinked.

He continued. "In Illinois. Where Joseph Smith got killed."

"Oh. So who cares?"

Cleon closed his eyes and sighed even harder. "The Church of Jesus Christ of Latter-day Saints, for one. Or, more specifically, the Forgotten King of Deseret and his family. *Quashquema* is the old, pre-Mormon name for Nauvoo, which used to be about the size of Chicago, and it's the town from whence Brigham Young led his frightened pilgrims to the Great Salt Lake Valley. It's also a stone's throw from Carthage, where the founder of their One True Faith was murdered—"

I interrupted. "Ah, right, their 'holy land.' Got it. And this guy . . ."

"This poor bastard we're meeting technically has claim to the area, at least metaphysically, despite the fact that he's never stepped foot into the 25th. His grandfather was a banker, a land owner, some grand muckety-muck in the Masons, and a respected member of AWAK back in his day. This kid is terrified of being gunned down by God's Watchdogs if he steps sideways. Or, I guess, if he breathes funny on this side of the curtain."

It was my turn to sigh. "So he's making us buy boarding passes for a flight we don't even want to take and meet him on the other side of a security checkpoint in a major multinational airport so that fanatical Mormons don't kill him as part of their weird, lemonade-drinking, whitebread jihad?"

Everyone stared at us.

Security guys started walking toward us.

Like I said, I hate airports.

Cleon sighed again. "Well, enjoy being detained. I'm going to go buy a soft pretzel and flirt with stewardesses. I'll tell the Third Earl of Quashquema you said 'hi.'"

"You tell him I said he's a fucking asshole!"

Cleon smirked and cleared his throat to use the Voice of Kings. "Got it. Sorry, officers—*he's not with me*."

"A fucking asshole! And I hope his plane crashes!"

On AWAK
and the Long Hour Holds

Clinton J. Boomer

More than once, I've been asked to describe the average Alone We Are Kings meeting—and those infamous Long Hour Hold soirees, held by what passes for a "community" amongst us totemic royalty.

These questions are mostly from total outsiders: people who've never actually been Sideways. Sometimes, of course, I'm queried by so-called *hourists* (tourists of the hour, like Tama) who've made the jump a few times and are curious about getting an invite to an AWAK formal event . . . and sometimes the question comes from particularly hermit-like occultists, who are old hats at the metaphysics of the nether, busy studying up to the point of claiming a little bit of totemic dirt and making themselves official royalty.

There are, it seems, plenty of folks out there who want to know what to expect if and when they meet up with fellow travelers in the 25th.

And they ask me all *manner* of questions.

This is usually because I'm known to be bluntly honest.

Unfortunately, oftentimes, my explanation doesn't seem to cut it. They simply won't take my word for it that AWAK is stupid and that it sucks and that everything about it—especially every event—is dumb and awful and not fucking worth it.

I am then often asked to elaborate.

So here's my official take on the subject.

Written down for posterity and everything.

My opinion is, of course, worth exactly what you paid for it; your mileage may vary, not available in all areas, void where prohibited, yadda yadda. One more disclaimer: any words uttered by the human tongue or penned by the human hand cannot begin to truly encompass the absolute weirdness that is the Impossible Hour or any section of it. My meager description and rude fumblings are incapable of conveying the utter insanity of what you'll see—and feel and hear and also experience using vibratory-magnetic, reptilian proto-senses you were not previously aware you had—the first time you attend a gathering at a Long Hour Hold.

Basically, if you get killed following my advice, please don't haunt me.

But I'll do my best to provide *some* type of guidance.

Allow me, then, to discuss and define the five "flavors" of the Alone We Are Kings community. These disparate and distinct parts of our intertwined pseudo-nations are each on proud display in a variety of fashions throughout any grouping of AWAK members, especially at a party. The more you know about them, the better.

I will, in a moment, ask you to imagine a pentagram cluster of five different possible scenarios—combining these elements in a variety of admixtures will give you a general sense of what you're stepping into.

As an aside, if you would like an illustration of how these five metaphorical flavors "mix," please feel free to perform the following science experiment. To make it fun, I'll be using drink making as the specific science in question because I spent a lot more time paying attention in bars than I ever did in a chemistry classroom.

Go grab a plastic cup.

Any size.

A cheapo one—not microwave safe or anything. Just something from a gas station or a fast food joint that's open all night. Don't bother to wash it out.

Add no ice. Ice will make it palatable. That is not the point of this.

Combine equal parts bottom-shelf mint schnapps, grapefruit juice, pelinkovec (it's a Slavic herbal liqueur; in a pinch, you can use warm Jägermeister that you've strained through a gym-sock), month-old goat milk, and Tabasco sauce.

Drop a dirty nickel in there.

Just one from the street or from behind a dumpster.

Mix thoroughly and nuke on high for ten seconds.

You will notice, once you smell the drink, that you can actually taste a distinct aroma of human bile. This is not a property of the hot, clotted liquid itself but is instead produced naturally by your own body.

Wow, right? Isn't science fun?

Yeah. So is magic. And in the same way.

Swallow it. Choke it down. Yeah.

This is the shit you're getting yourself into.

Now that we're ready, what *are* the five "flavors" of AWAK? They are, in no particular order, as follows:

- ❖ Madhouse, Starving Addicts
- ❖ Power-Hungry Deviants
- ❖ Dangerously Weird Obsessives
- ❖ Illogical Inhumans, Insane Immortals, and their Fetishists
- ❖ and, of course, the Lonely Freaks

I fit into that last category, in case you were wondering.

And also maybe the Dangerously Weird Obsessives one, too.

There's some overlap is what I'm saying.

So what should you expect when you walk in the door of the Long Hour Hold, announce your Kingdom at the top of your lungs, take off your pants, and accept a still-flaming drink from an old woman dressed as a puppy?

Madhouse, Starving Addicts

Imagine an inner-city homeless shelter on Christmas Eve if they were offering double portions of beef stew and a free bag of meth to the first one hundred people to show up in a cape, assless leather chaps, or blue face paint or with a visible tattoo of a cartoon character having sex with an animal.

Now imagine that there is apparently an ongoing, rules-free fistfight occurring in the back of the room—right next to the soda machines inexplicably selling bottles of laudanum and the tears of preteens—over the topic of which episode of *Golden Girls* had the most veiled allusions to the Illuminati/Reptilian shadow government.

Imagine that this is where your blind date asked you to meet her.

Power-Hungry Deviants

Imagine a slick, high-quality, mob-run Japanese steakhouse with sleek glass and steel décor in a trendy, bohemian part of town. The sort of place where you put on a suit and tie just to call up and make reservations. The restaurant is exclusive, quiet, understated, underground, top-notch, and hosted in a quaint, one-hundred-year-old walk-up loft that—due to some strange translation error—is hung entirely with found art from burned-down churches and abandoned children's hospitals.

Imagine that this place has a dimly lit, muted-neon bar in the back where grim, wealthy men are served sushi, live octopus, and uncut cocaine off of naked geisha girls . . . and that it is hung with banners for a pirate-themed professional cricket team from a town in Lithuania you've never heard of.

Now imagine that everyone here is wearing rubber animal masks, and every single person in the room can shoot lasers and fly.

Imagine that you are here to meet a guy who is willing to sell you actual hair taken from the burned scalp of Michael Jackson.

Dangerously Weird Obsessives

Imagine a rain-washed, run-down 1970s biker bar and honkytonk strip club, sitting in the disused corner of a gravel truckstop parking lot next to an empty field along the interstate—the sort of place where the signs reading "Thanks For Not Smoking" and "No Shirt, No Shoes, No Service" have been replaced, respectively, with "Do Not Spit Chewed-Up Cigar Butts Directly Into My Face or I Will Knife You" and "If You Are Bleeding From the Nipples, Please Keep Your Blood Off The Bar."

Imagine the sort of place where you piss in a long metal trough, which may or may not be in the bathroom; the sort of place where it's okay to throw beer bottles as long as they don't actually *hit* anybody . . . or, at least, anybody bigger, meaner, or better armed than you; the sort of place where one of the waitresses is observably pregnant, may or may not be out of her early teens, and who has to keep telling rowdy customers that if they don't stop pinching her, her dad will kick their asses—he's sitting right over there next to the jukebox, ya'll.

Now imagine that, although a significant portion of the customers are cowboys, truckers, and blue-collar types, around half the clientele are inexplicably dressed as 17th-century French aristocracy. And that some of the dancers are Filipino boys dressed as maids. And instead of pool tables and dartboards, a loud segment of the rowdy drinkers is clustered around a massive hardcover book of technical drawings by Tesla, arguing loudly about its relationship to Dante's *Inferno*.

Imagine that some of those technical drawings are of non-existent automobile/aero-gyro hybrids and that one guy is openly masturbating.

Imagine that this is the place you come to relax.

Illogical Inhumans, Insane Immortals and their Fetishists

Imagine a massive comic book convention on cosplay Saturday, featuring in grand abundance the sorts of uber-nerds who go to renaissance festivals dressed as Klingons; Vulcans; Rinax-born, Borg-assimilated Talaxians; and assorted other non-human cast members of Star Trek. For every semi-recognizable costume—even of something as obscure as a fetishized Jedi Muppet, a sidekick robot from the Kamen Rider/Ultraman crossover cartoon, or a steampunk Pikachu hybrid of one of the Doctors from *Doctor Who*—there are a dozen guys in painstakingly elaborate getups from something truly alien with inspiration apparently taken from 1700s Dutch sci-fi comic books, background characters from particularly high-budget Turkish action films never released in the States, or Monty Python sketches that somehow never made it past the "Graham Chapman has a feverish nightmare and forgets to write it down" stage.

Now imagine that, at one point, you bump into a woman in a "rubber sexy anime angel-nurse-biker-whore" costume, and it turns out that it's *not* a costume. And that her boyfriend, who *looks* to be a four-hundred-pound, bald quadriplegic with papier-mâché dragon limbs superglued to his shoulders and hips and with a face tattoo proclaiming him to be "DJ Jay-Jay Ray-Ray," has superstrength, fire breath, and a desire to try midget tossing.

Because only like *half* of the people here are technically "dressed up."

And some of them are "dressed" as people.

Imagine that the rest—like that catgirl wearing half a chainmail bikini or the guy with no face openly fingering her—are not human and never have been and don't want to be. Now imagine that about 10% of the people here are flat-out, heart-stoppingly *gorgeous*. Truly, deeply, eye-wateringly beautiful, to a point of unrealism—not like professional models, but just a few steps past that. Like a Photoshop of a Photoshop of the most beautiful wet dream you've ever had. At least a quarter of the room pings your "uncanny valley" sensor at first sight and just won't stop. Also, this is apparently the type of community wherein it is simply generally accepted that a certain measurable percentage of the population is sexually attracted to weasels and that Nazi fetishism is also fine. This is the sort of place that kids really *don't* belong, but you keep spotting grown adults walking around with toddlers and teenagers, and in some cases, it's not entirely clear that they're not a dating couple. There are open, live steel weapons, and non-comical duels wherein people are actually getting bitten and stabbed, and you've seen at least two people engaging in what *can't* be consensual sex with that third person.

If there is any type of event staff or security, those people are apparently on their smoke break. Speaking of smoke, there are a dozen or more open flames and people dancing around them to something that is very much musicless.

Now imagine that this convention is taking place in what used to be a high-rise, assisted-living apartment complex back during WWII but that it has since been gutted, grafted onto an old grain silo, and turned into something halfway between a parking garage, a roller rink, and a series of quite structurally unsound ballrooms . . . all with a glowing "swimming pit" at the very bottom.

Imagine that this is where the messiah of the new cult you've just joined first met your awesome new deity, and he sent you here to reconnect with Her estranged kid . . . violently, if necessary.

The Lonely Freaks

Imagine a junior high dance for a Catholic school on the last week before Christmas break . . . in a community so awkward and ugly that Steve Buscemi would be considered a really good-looking guy.

Or girl, honestly.

Imagine that this is like that school out of your anxiety nightmares where some students don't graduate until they're in their thirties.

Imagine that, because of a sudden, pressing need to fumigate the actual school over break, the dance is being held in a bleak, rundown Jewish funeral home right down the road. Now imagine that, due to a simultaneous flu outbreak, several house fires, and a blizzard, no chaperones showed up except one drunken physics teacher who is having an affair with two of his students.

Imagine that this is the sort of dance where everyone was told that they could dress however they wanted, but nobody's parents believed them, so everyone in attendance is wearing weird, smuggled-in props over ill-fitting formal wear. Imagine that several of the attendees are swigging from hip flasks and that the mood is turning sour as the DJ plays his music at ever-increasing volumes.

Imagine that in this school, due to a weird loophole in district-wide policy, anyone can start a club for any reason and that the president of each club is given several hundred dollars a month to spend however he or she sees fit. Also, each competing chess club or anime fandom is allowed their own private use of one room in the school for an hour a day for "club activities." Imagine that this has led to a weird, tribal fracturing of the student body to a point that everyone mistrusts everyone else, and the various clubs are in a protracted Cold War of internecine feuds.

Imagine that within this society the most powerful people are the ones committed to organizing the clubs—the yearbook team is at the throats of the student council, and they are conspiring against the lurking danger of the pan-athletic boosters who are ready to strike down the choral department.

Imagine that everyone is laughing at the tuxedo-wearing, 120-pound kid sitting in the corner playing a Japanese trading card game with a 400-pound girl wrapped in sea-foam-green taffeta—only, it's because he's left his back to the assassins.

Now imagine that this school is the place where your insane, now-dead great-uncle used to teach European history and that to get the inheritance he left you, you have to blackmail the head of the cheerleaders. Revealing that she once fellated a live wolverine at a party won't work because everyone knows that.

Those are our five flavors.

If that hasn't driven you away, then . . . welcome to AWAK, I suppose. See you at the Long Hour Hold. Bring your own protection.

I'll be the drunken midget in the back, shouting obscenities at everyone.

Meet the Forgotten
King of Saigon

Clinton J. Boomer

I hate meeting with forgotten royalty.

But more than that, I hate *trying to get* meetings with forgotten royalty.

It's like these people have never heard of a fucking appointment book.

I'm there sitting in my underwear on a dinged-up, paper-covered "massage" table like something out of a horror-show, back-alley clinic in a low-budget 70s exploitation flick at three in the morning in a Vietnamese whorehouse in the middle of a strip mall on the wrong side of Vegas, and I happen to notice that my life just keeps getting worse with each passing day.

Cheesy, tinny, faux-Asian music is tinkling over the loudspeakers, not quite cranked up enough to drown out the spatter and patter of the neon-lit, decorative fountains stuck in every corner, and I can vaguely hear the mama-san at the front desk slowly losing her temper as she argues with a drunken prospective client. He's raving about how he doesn't want to have to wear a condom. And he's doing it just angrily enough, is my guess, to make the off-duty, plainclothes cop providing security in the lobby slightly uncomfortable.

Somewhere farther down the hallway—back here in the "private area"—two people are shouting violently at each other in a language I don't understand (probably a very obscure dialect of Nguồn), and someone else is sobbing.

I can hear a fat middle manager from some farm-equipment insurance company in Omaha getting blown by a disinterested, illegal immigrant teenager.

The two of them are in the room right next door.

Everything here stinks of hand lotion, spermicidal lubricant, and cheap incense.

I need a drink. And a cigarette. And a new, very different life.

Cleon nudges me. "Take off your shoes."

He's sitting next to me on the massage table, also in his underwear. His shoes, shirt, and pants are off, but he's still wearing those stupid blue and red 3D glasses.

"I'm not taking off my shoes. The floors here are disgusting."

He leans back and shrugs. "Suit yourself. But don't blame me when you have to explain why you don't have your shoes off."

"What, are they going to totally freak out that I have my shoes on? Is that some part of Vietnamese whorehouse culture that I wasn't aware off?"

Cleon shrugs again. "Kinda. It's considered rude."

I fold my arms over my chest. "Well, I want them on in case I have to sprint out of here or kick someone in the face. And I'm not touching this horrible, disgusting floor with my bare feet."

He nods. "Yeah. That's sort of why it's considered rude."

The door opens suddenly, and a girl slips in.

Cleon and I both look up just in time to see a well-dressed, angry young man walk past, heading to the front desk to deal—physically, probably—with either the drunk, the madam, the security-guy/cop, or all three.

The door closes softly.

The woman—a beautiful someone we haven't seen before—turns and starts to say something very politely. She stops mid-sentence as she gets a look at us.

In her defense, Cleon and I are something of a sight.

Especially sitting there in our underwear.

She does her best not to gawk at us.

I give her credit for that.

Cleon speaks up, overenunciating and gesturing at my shoes. "I'm very sorry that my friend is so rude. He is quite nervous. This is his first time meeting such pretty girls."

The woman regains her composure and feigns a sympathetic—and slightly seductive—smile. "Ah. You both ready for massage?"

I can tell she's had a long night. My heart goes out to her. It really does.

I speak up. "Oh, yes. But I'm so nervous . . . do you have anything to help me, uh . . . calm my nerves?"

She narrows her eyes at me. "No. Massage very calming."

I put on my most innocent face. "I, uh . . . the cabbie told us that Mr. . . . *Huynh*, is it? That someone named Huynh might have *something* to help me relax. And to, uh . . . *enjoy myself.*"

She narrows her eyes at me even further.

I give her my best grin and hold up a wad of hundreds.

She relaxes and smiles, and I can tell how pretty she is when she isn't doing this stupid, awful job. "Of course. I be right back. You get . . . comfortable."

Like a shadow, she slips back out of the room.

Cleon nudges me. "She means to take off your shoes."

"Shut up. I don't care. So—step one, complete. What's next?"

He shrugs again. I hate how calm he is. "If you didn't spook her already, next we meet the dealer. If the bouncer at the Beaten Path was telling the truth, we pass heroin-guy a few bucks and ask him about the gambling. Play our cards right, and we get to see the back room. We place a few bets, have a few beers, pass the pit boss a few *more* bucks, and then, we ask about the human trafficking."

I roll my eyes. "Ugh. This sucks. And then?"

Cleon shrugs again. "Then, we're at the last step. Keep cool, seem legit, and we get to meet the Forgotten King of Saigon. And then we can ask him about Lethal Thrust, Inc., and that's it."

"And then we can get out of this stupid, neon-plastic bullshit town?"

Cleon nods noncommittally. "Sure."

"I hate this."

He nods again. "That's if all goes well, of course. If not, then . . ."

"*Then*, what?"

Cleon shows his nervousness for the first time. I could kiss him for it. "Bad stuff. *Then*, we have to get out of here alive, and we go back tomorrow night during the Nether Hour and whip the ever-living shit out of the bouncer at the Beaten Path."

I grin for the first time in what seems like ages. "He's pretty big."

Cleon shrugs again, smiling. "All bluster, no bite. You can tell by the *Mom* tattoo on his neck."

"I think that's supposed to be intimidating. And it was a picture of *your* mom, after all."

"He's a pushover. I'll grab him by the unicorn horn. You punch him in the whatever he has instead of balls until he stops moving."

That actually gets a laugh out of me. But I remember where we are. "You know, I really do hate this."

My best friend nods. "Yeah. You know, we could have gone the weapons-buying route. But you didn't want anyone pointing an AK at your face."

"You didn't want it, either."

He nods again. "Yeah. You'd go shithouse."

I chuckle without much mirth.

We sit in silence for a while.

Finally, I pipe up again. "So why is this bastard so careless with his insane paranoia?"

Cleon frowns. "What do you mean?"

I sigh and throw up my hands in exasperation. "The asshole who runs this place is too scared of the Forgotten King of Prey Nokor to step into the 25th. He doesn't take visitors. He doesn't go out in public. That part I totally get. But as a "solution" to the problem, he's got a massage parlor, inexplicably open for business and lit up like the Fourth of July in the middle of a strip mall between a shuttered Mexican grocery store and an abandoned nail salon. This place is the front for like five different shell corporations of increasing illegality between him and the real world."

"Yeah?"

I blink at him. "So anyone who *really* wanted to tag this dumb French bastard could just bulldoze the place. Firebomb it. Show up at eleven in the morning on a Sunday, when he's sleeping it off, with a few dozen pounds of high explosives and just burn the place to the ground."

"I'm sure he's thought of that."

"Sure. Maybe. I'm just saying that these forgotten royalty assholes sure don't seem to have much fear of—or respect for—us little guys."

For a moment, it looks like Cleon is going to say something. Then he doesn't. After a pause, he inhales. Finally, he just nods and says, "Yeah."

I smirk. "What? You were going to say, 'big shock—that's what makes them forgotten,' or something?"

He shakes his head and smirks back. "Naw. I was *going* to say that's what makes them royalty."

I harrumph.

We sit in silence a little longer.

The fat insurance guy next door finally gets done getting blown. We listen to him awkwardly putting his pants back on as his latest paid conquest goes somewhere presumably to wash her mouth out with turpentine.

I idly wonder what ever happened to that drunken guy at the front. All is quiet except for the crappy music and the burble of the fountains.

I want to kind of hum along, but I resist.

Cleon starts to fidget. He checks his watch. "God damn, how long is it going to take this heroin dealer?"

This time, I'm the one who gets to shrug noncommittally. "I'm sure it's a busy night."

"Sure. Lots of customers."

I grin. "People like massages and heroin and white slavery—it's the American dream. Hey, how much money will you give me if I tell the heroin dealer that the unholy magic of human sacrifice along the Saigon River flows in my veins before I flying tackle him?"

Cleon punches me in the shoulder. "Nothing, asshole. You know, talking like that is—"

And that's when the door comes crashing open, and several armed men rush in and try to kill us.

As I leap at the first one and try to push him backward into his friend, I'm glad I kept my shoes on—although Cleon is too busy setting another guy on fire to notice.

Like I say, I hate meeting with forgotten royalty.

On Spirit Creatures

Clinton J. Boomer

People ask me, sometimes, why I hate spirit critters so damn much.

These people are mostly assholes.

This type of question is usually, I should note, not *really* a question at all. It's just an invitation to an argument and, occasionally, to a fistfight, and on one memorable occasion, it served as an entrance into a long-winded villain monologue by a big guy named Klark with an arm made out of devil teeth who was only a few minutes—by his estimation—from blowing a very large hole in my undersized skull using an exceptionally huge handgun made from severed penises that shot sticky, chocolate-syrup-covered maggots at hypersonic speed.

That one didn't end well for him.

He still walks with a limp, last I heard.

And that magic handgun wound up vanishing, which *really* pissed me off. The thing kept giggling at me and making very suggestive, sodomy-related threats.

My hope that it won't show up again lies in the fact that only someone with significantly superhuman strength could lift it—it was bigger than my torso. Seriously. I don't even know where you would get that many severed penises.

But every once in great while, the whole "spirit critter hate" thing really *is* honestly a question. An innocent query. The sort of thing you ask a guy over a beer. Or casually bring up when meeting an interesting stranger on a transatlantic flight. Or mention to break the tension after you're done fucking and lighting up that post-coital smoke in an off-ramp hotel room.

"So, tell me, why do you hate spirit creatures?"

Not far from "So how's your night treating you?" or "What do you do for a living?" or "So . . . you come here often?" And, as a question, it's a damn sight more pleasant than "What's the weather like down there?" or "Are you all deformed and stuff because, you know, like, your mom drank when she was pregnant and stuff?"

And when it really is an honest question, I sincerely don't mind answering.

But asking me why I carry such a grudge against the fairytale creatures among us, unfortunately, is like asking why I hate the Irish.

Oh, well gee, let me fucking *count* the reasons. Where to start? Because they're so willfully stupid? Or because they're so insufferably arrogant? Or because they're generally a lot of mean-spirited bullies who think recognizing cognitive dissonance is "for fags"? Or because, to a man, they're all a bunch of loud, racist, drunken, short-tempered, misogynistic pricks apparently born with an encyclopedic knowledge of short jokes? Or because the dumb yahoos are forever looking for their next excuse to punch someone in the throat?

And, might I add, the Irish are even worse.

And no one wants to hear that.

My so-called peer group is composed almost entirely of people with hard-ons to hang out with spirit critters, borrow their superpowers, and have kinky sex with them. Hell, half the guys trolling the Nether Time for cheap laughs, illogical alcoholic beverages, and weird, furry tail are the "token human" amongst what they like to think of as their friends.

Which brings me to an important note: spirit creatures don't actually like you.

You are not their friend.

You are, at best, someone they haven't killed yet.

But the point is—in summation—that my views are observably in the minority amongst Alone We Are Kings.

Which means I often get into arguments. And fistfights. And have to hear long-winded villain monologues.

And so the question stands: "Why do I hate spirit creatures so much?"

Let me tell you since you're so insistent.

Some people figure that I must just hate all non-humans.

That couldn't be further from the truth. I love dogs, and there are several cats I get along with just fine, and my buddy Jerome and his boyfriend Devin used to have a little Vietnamese pot-bellied pig named Sooie-Sue Sudio who was so sweet and so smart and so cute that I actually cried at her funeral.

She always gave me little Sooie-Sue kisses and made snorting noises when she was being silly. Dammit, I'm actually getting a little choked up thinking about that.

Also, I tolerate fish just fine.

I cannot, for the life of me, imagine keeping fish as pets—mostly because they don't strike me as particularly "cuddly" or "fun" or "useful as a substitute for human companionship without the bullshit," and that's what I'm looking for in a pet . . . but they're generally pretty inoffensive. Perhaps a little high maintenance for the payoff, and sometimes, they smell weird, but the same could be said of houseplants or Pokémon enthusiasts. And I don't have any real problem with them.

And let's remember, I also hate the Irish, and they're still categorized as people, last I checked.

No, I hate creatures from the 25th for much more specific reasons that have nothing to do with humanocentrism.

But in order to get into that, you're gonna have to bear with me on this for a moment.

So there's a weird old lateral-thinking test that Google used to use during interviews for potential new employees. It's the sort of thing that is supposed to test how well you can devise clever solutions to odd problems. It involves eight very nearly identical spheres and the weighing thereof.

It's a relatively famous logic/math problem. If you already know this one, feel free to skip ahead, and please, don't shout out the answer to everybody.

Here's the gist.

You've got eight spheres, all of them seemingly identical. Maybe they're the size of ping-pong balls; maybe they're the size of oranges. Doesn't matter. The point is that they're all basically indistinguishable in all ways measurable by humans: same diameter, same temperature, same response to being smashed by a hammer, all the good stuff.

One of them just happens to weigh slightly more than the others. Like, a ten-thousandth of an ounce. Nothing that you can feel in hand or that it revealed when you toss them down an elevator shaft, but *just* enough to show up on a scale that's calibrated to be accurate down to a billionth of an ounce.

You also have one of those incredible scales.

So that's cool.

The puzzle is this: how do you figure out which of the balls is heaviest if you only use that scale *twice*?

Now, it's pretty obvious how you would do it if you could use the scale four times: divide the eight spheres into four pairs of two, then compare the pairs.

If you can use the scale three times, I bet you could figure out a way you would do it, too.

My way—just so you know—would be to divide the eight into two groups of four and compare those; divide the heavier four into two pairs of two and compare those; and weigh the last, heaviest two against one another.

Ta-da!

The hard part, then, is noodling out how to do it in just two.

Just two moves.

Think about it for a second.

Honest to god, there really is a solution. I couldn't come up with it, even after hammering my skull about it for a half hour, and I've never seen anyone come up with it completely and 100% on their own . . . but somebody might have done it.

As an aside, the closest I've ever seen to watching the solution unfold was when a pair of very smart buddies of mine—one of them a composition and rhetoric professor who moonlights as a strategic military advisor to a certain shapeshifting demon lord who is not to be named, the other buddy a heavily tattooed fry cook—cracked it between the two of them. The three of us sat in a coffee shop for like an hour. They drew pictures and argued briefly and repeatedly told me that I was a dick (which I am), and eventually, they came up with exactly the right answer and in the right way, for the right reasons, and using problem-solving techniques that I really should have written down. It was incredibly cool, actually.

It made me pretty proud. I considered blogging about it.

But the point is that there does not exist a single spirit creature in the whole universe that would ever come up with the solution by *thinking about it*.

Not because they're stupid. Some of them are very smart. But they don't share our psychology.

Every one of the cheating fucks who agreed to take the test would pull some bullshit. Like by asking the inanimate spheres themselves which one of them was the heaviest or by ensorcelling the guy who asked the question to make him think they had solved it. Or through aura-reading the scale while holding up each of the balls to it and waiting for the right combo. Or even just travelling backward in time after testing each possible permutation and claiming that there was only a single "true" balance test—in this fork of reality, anyway—and therefore they "got it in one."

Because all spirit creatures are dirty cheaters.

They brute-force and workaround everything.

That's half of why I don't like them.

But it's not the whole reason. I honestly have no problem with dirty cheaters, in general. I'm one of that ill-reputed crew, too: there's no way, playing by the rules of the grand game as written that all other—read as "non-magical"—people follow, that I should be anywhere *nearly* as dangerous as I am in a fight.

Or as good at breaking handcuffs.

Or quite so capable of teleporting.

I cheat constantly and reflexively.

So do most of the people I know.

And I've been accused of brute-forcing (or workarounding) a few solutions myself over the years.

No, it's not just the cheating that gets to me.

The other half of the hatred equation (hatequation?) is that spirit creatures are smugly self-superior *because* of this ability to not have to think.

They imagine we're stupid and weak because we don't have immortality and mind control and flight and superstrength and the magic power to shoot lasers. And the idea that we might be as good as them because—even without *all* of that, we still have civilization and invented pants and don't constantly choke to death on our own tongues . . . well, that idea just makes them laugh.

They laugh and laugh and pat you on the head.

If you happen to screw up and admit that you think humans are actually *better* than the fae and the demons and the gremlins and the like . . . well, get ready to get punched in the face.

And don't say I didn't warn you.

End of It All: On the Farthest of the Far Sideways

Clinton J. Boomer

The box at our door, it turned out, contained the severed head of our "inside man." There was a note in his mouth. I'll paraphrase and just say that it was quite rude and that the author spent most of it referring to us as homosexuals.

At that point, we were shit out of luck and powerfucked for options.

What we needed, it was decided—over a third pot of bad coffee as the sun finally came up, Cleon pacing with his fists clenched, muttering obscenities, and me trying semi-futilely to smoke a cigarette without taking my forehead off the table—was to talk to someone outside spacetime as we understood it.

Someone with a truly, finally, and absolutely—above all—*different* perspective on the situation.

Someone more deeply, assuredly sideways than even the *farthest* Far Sideways.

Someone not on the payroll of any player, now or then or *ever*.

Someone literally *beyond* good and evil.

That decided, Cleon and I stared at each other for a few moments, each of us trying to decide if the other one was literally suggesting the insane and impossible. We each made some phone calls, and we checked out of the fleabag motel before 9:00 a.m., made a few last pickups, and started driving.

We were headed, no bullshit, for a conference with one of the Formless.

This required several steps in preparation for trying something that a lot of people talked about doing and that no one—to my knowledge—ever actually *did*.

First step: protection.

Cleon's guy, Stav, turned out to be a greasy fellow in a bright white jean jacket who chain-smoked Kool cigarettes and owned what I took to be an abandoned airplane hangar. He re-cut a pair of decommissioned cosmonaut suits while we waited, after which he offered to sell us (a) some very weird Eastern European porn by the pound, (b) some hairpieces made from "real tiger fur, my friends," and (c) a five-chambered, semiautomatic revolver that fired 7.62-millimeter M1943 Soviet rifle rounds and that he swore was "good for 25th stuff."

He was getting rid of it because it could be detected with a Geiger counter, but he claimed that it fired even in vacuum. Since Stav was willing to trade in stolen watches and half a carton of Camels, he made a sale.

Everything except the hairpieces. We didn't want those.

Cleon and I were now half-done with step one.

It was time to begin step two: a bribe for our new Formless contact.

I won't go into how we got our hands on a bottle of ambrosia because the last thing I want is any of you assholes getting bright ideas and trying to duplicate our oh-so-clever efforts, but long story short, we stole it.

We had absolutely no proof that this bribe would in any way work, of course . . . but if there's one thing that powerful creatures pretty much universally like, it's ambrosia. And the theory was that if everything went tits-up and to shit, simultaneously, we could at least drink the stuff before we died.

So back to finishing up step one. As I'm sure you know, getting to Deseret is a giant pain the ass, and dealing with the racist-ass Forgotten Kings squatting on the Sideways reflection of the property all around the Great Salt Lake is decidedly *less* pleasant still. But there's simply no one on the planet currently producing better abjuration magic than those paranoid dickholes, so that's where we headed . . . with a pair of recently retrofitted, lead-lined spacesuits stuffed in the trunk next to my new gun and a bottle of alcohol with a dollar value hovering somewhere just above "priceless."

A quick stop in Carthage, Illinois—at the historic jail where Joseph Smith was martyred—marked the beginning of the next leg of the trip. It's the only way to get on the One True Path to Deseret. I'll admit, for a town with less than three thousand people and a history of religiously motivated lynching, it's actually pretty nice. They have both a Hardee's and a Dairy Queen. There's also an amazingly cute winery right outside of town. It's rustic without seeming either plasticky or rundown, and the cheese and cracker platter is really good. The people at the desk told me they make personalized labels for bottles, and I strongly considered ordering one of me flipping off the camera, Johnny Cash style, and calling it Suck My Midget Dick Merlot or something.

Would have made a great gift for Tama & Garrick's wedding.

Unfortunately, I didn't have any money on me, and Cleon was keeping his credit card under closer watch than I was hoping, so it was a no go.

The two of us walked around the lake at the winery, fed the ducks, and talked out our next move. We decided that, yes, we were actually going insane.

I also checked to see if there was a strip club in town. I was disappointed to hear that the answer was an emphatic *no*.

A crooked, half-hour drive north-northwest got us to Nauvoo. For a town of less than twelve hundred people, it's *not* very nice. According to the pamphlet I stole, it was home to a French socialist utopian commune in the 1850s, after the locals drove the Mormons out, and by the 1900s (and through about 2002), it was almost entirely controlled by the Roman Catholics. They can keep it, as far as I'm concerned . . . although I guess the LDS doesn't see it that way because they own most of the town now.

They *also* did not have a strip club.

From there, it was across the river at midnight and into the 25th and a long, lonely drive into the nether version of the West.

The trail, trial, and travel into the desert takes forty days and forty nights, according to some legends, and closer to forty years, depending on who you talk to . . . but Miss Molly goes a hell of a lot faster than people do. Or than sound does, technically. It wasn't an hour before we were in sight of the great wood-walled compounds of the many zealous separatist Kings of Deseret, each under his own particular banner of heaven, each striving like the dickens to claim his spot in the Celestial Kingdom.

Assholes, every last one of them.

My smoking didn't go over at *all*.

Getting full-length, body-hugging magical Mormon underwear with which to line the inside of our spacesuits, layering on a set for all eight days of the week (including the secret one), and having every thread of the things blessed, sanctified, baptized, and anointed with holy oils . . . that was something of an ordeal although not a particularly interesting one.

Cleon and I were each called "foul, godless Lamanites" several more times than I think was entirely called for.

Once we threatened, cajoled, and bargained with the least racist Capital Household of the Forgotten Empire of Deseret (that was King Bill, of the Fundamentalist Orthodox Reform Western Arizona branch of the empire, for the record) for what we wanted and dealt with all seven hundred of his wives, all three hundred of his concubines, and *way* more conservative blond, teenage boys with assault rifles than I ever want to see again, it was another long drive . . . even more crooked, strange, and deep into the far-westmost Sideways.

I'm not sure how long we drove after that; the sun stopped coming up, and the clocks had been funny since we crossed the Mississippi.

We put our protective gear on just as the asphalt was starting to boil and the air was turning to methane's evil cousin.

First, we each donned a wreath of seven enchanted Betamax medallions, the eight sets of magical Mormon underwear, another five tapes on top, the spacesuits, and a final layer of thirteen more medallions. This added up, of course, to several days of 25th Hour protection apiece to keep us safe.

In theory.

In practice, we looked like ridiculous ancient aliens piloting a flying convertible across a postmodern, glitch-ridden version of a Salvador Dali painting rendered in colors that should not be.

But we didn't burst into flames and die, so that was somewhat reassuring.

The various conversations between me and Cleon ended at around that point, too. The suits were equipped with radios, but the electromagnetic spectrum started having fits.

Eventually, we had to leave Miss Molly behind, so we walked into the rapidly breaking wasteland.

I'd really like to be able to explain why that was necessary, precisely, but the physics of the place was fucked up enough that I might as well say both that "we had to go into an odd jungle cave" and also that "we had to climb the side of a mountain, which was also a river, but going up."

After a few more days or maybe weeks, we passed through the shadow of a castle that looked like something a seven-year-old would draw if she were sketching out a portrait of the place where true evil lived. They were having a very loud orgy inside, and we snuck by. We followed some train tracks for a while until they stopped running in parallel and started doing loops and sketching out very phallic roses. A while after that, we came to a sheer, thundering cliff face running up from the earth all the way to the sky. We shimmied through a crack and clambered down a massive pipe in the dark. We had to swim for a while in something that wasn't water.

There were ghosts.

I found myself looking up and seeing the bottoms of trees, roads, and buildings rooted into the sky and staring at the foundation pillars of some higher universe hanging there in the black.

We got to a place that might have been a cavern or a maze, or it might have been outdoors in a place that was still booting up from bad programming. We pushed by and found some halls where old eons are stored in crystal, one save state after another. After that, it seemed normal for a while: long stretches of bruise-colored sky, ringed by purple hills along avenues of blue-and-gold plaid houses in a burning suburb on a hot fall day.

At this point, I would like to apologize to you, the reader, because I don't think I'm doing a very good job describing the deepest Sideways at *all*.

I find that I have to say things like, "there was this specific instance where we were walking on the side of an office building frozen in mid-fall across a field made of a time-stopped ultra-tsunami hitting a major 22nd-century city, except that the center of gravity was shifted 45 degrees to the southeast. Anyway, halfway across the thing, it started raining severed human body parts, except that, instead of falling, they were coming in from another dimension and intersecting our plane of existence at right angles, so they were blipping in and out in torrents: first the marrow, then the bone, then the blood, then the skin— and by that point the marrow would be gone again—and then the screaming.

"Also, it was all in the shape of the inside of a knot."

Which is stupid. I feel like I ought to be inflicting this babble on somebody who really deserves it rather than on you. So . . . I'm sorry.

A lot of places also had things fused into one another: machines buried into hard-packed soil and speared through by poles and wires or stacked in endless pillars of intermingled layers of glass, iron, and concrete and stacked in lattices.

Anyway, it was claustrophobic and hot and dark, like a feverish nightmare about being lost and trapped in a steam tunnel under the swimming pool of an abandoned mental institution for kids.

The feeling of vertigo grew stronger and stronger, never abating.

By the end, I was sweating and shaking and puking. Tears streamed from my eyes, unable to focus because of the blinking. Mucus and blood ran freely from my nose and dripped down my chest, and I drooled, slack-jawed, as I pissed myself.

We came around something like a corner—although we did not turn left or right.

And there it was. Beyond us and all around us—as if looking up and out from the bottom of a bucket as it's kicked down the stairs—there was something very evocative of a horizon . . . but without a "line" or a "curve" even tangentially involved.

It was the edge.

The edge.

What we were *not*, I assure you, was "at the low, crashing end of a long river canyon run beneath a towering, impossible, night-lit refinery, watching the last spills of the one fluid reality I had as yet perceived sputter, twist, and flow outward and down (and up and into) the waterfall of another, more alien universe, grinding the immense and improbable wheel of a great machine all around us, half in and half out of both time and space. I saw the bubble in all ten dimensions."

But, shit . . . that's probably the closest I'm gonna get to describing it.

My head hurt, now vibrating with a frequency inexpressible in our continuum, and the suit around me started fraying and burning. Gravity was splashing back and forth at my feet and began running in rivulets up my chest.

I heard Cleon tap on my helmet.

I turned, and he pointed.

There was a . . . *something*, which I couldn't quite see, on the other side of a border—which I also couldn't quite see—waiting for us. It was bathed in light that I now remember as livid purple, though at the time I thought it was greenish grey, and it stuttered into view like a sea anemone on fast rewind as seen by an epileptic.

It was *not* a tree, and it was not a starfish. It wasn't a shifting wave of sharp-edged prisms strung along cords like a marionette being thrown down an elevator shaft, and it also wasn't a collection of colon tumors seen in x-ray, all overlapping.

Gun to my head, I would say it reminded me of a blurry black-and-white photo of an old elm tree in winter, ghastly stark in shadow and sunlight alike, run through about thirty thousand different filters on a cheap, error-prone knock off of Photoshop by a spastic with no grasp of aesthetics.

But that's not to say it didn't also look like an inside-out, upside-down kraken, too.

The "matter" it was composed of seemed to be coils of infinite, thinly stretched black garbage bags full of hot puke and cold kitty litter, pulled so taut in some places that you could make out the seams of manufacturing defects in the plastic, and all spinning without going anywhere.

It wasn't standing on anything, but it wasn't hanging in space, either. It was clutched to the precipice of another world, tethered to something that now registers in my brain as simply an untranslatable well of static and gibberish.

The thing in the doorway stared at us—or, I suppose, I felt as though it was staring.

It had something I might have called a head although it wasn't pointing at me. The nostril-like "eyes" dotted around it weren't all pointing in my direction.

It spoke.

That was the worst part of the whole trip.

Imagine, as an aside, that instead of living in your house or apartment or whatever, you were a deep-sea organism: one dwelling in the watery interior of a mega-planet-sized, ice-covered moon orbiting a super-Jovian gas giant lit dimly from within by a spinning metal core and the molten oceans of magma and dirty water forever surrounding it.

Instead of gazing, each night, toward the stars above, you spend your endless days looking "up" at a sun that never moves: a fission-powered storm of magnetism, lightning, and reddish thunder, roiling at the center of a mass of blackish, liquescent, super-heated steam hot enough to flash-fry uranium and dense enough to crush an aircraft carrier like an empty pack of cigarettes. The tectonics of your planet create occasional god-sized whirlpools into the "depths" as temperature differentials spray geysers of your oceanic home out onto the unknowable, inhospitable moon surface far "below."

Your clouds "above" are the super-heated vents of the core, spraying liquid iron "down" into the cold mega-sea that is your home, raining back "up" as veins of dense volcanic glass intermingled with studs of diamond and gold.

Innumerable creatures of titanic size and brute-simple evolution graze in long sheets and ribbons upon this eternal, dancing chemosynthetic bounty in the sky above you—or burn and die and tumble "upward" into the uncaring storm.

You, "below," drift through the weird currents that run between the nameless peaks of icy mountains hanging "up" into this world. You scuttle and swoop over the rents that lead "down" into eternally darkened, pressureless valleys where whitish crab rays prey on flat-bodied worms, hunting across fields of dangling black kelp lace.

This sealed ocean world, half-again bigger than Earth, would be too vast for you to ever truly explore. The sections of the planet hospitable to your species would be wide, encompassing in cubic meters a thousand-thousand times more than the square footage of Earth's meager surface, and containing vast drifting islands of complex organic matter ten times the size of our continents.

This would be a place without meteor strikes or stargazing, the living core of your ever-turbulent world shielded forever from the cold vacuum of hard space and the baking radiation of its weird parent by miles upon miles of hard-packed ice.

That is *not* what the Formless Magistrate's voice sounded like.

Imagine that humans came to your home.

They burrow "up" from the thin, dead cold at the "bottom" of the world, cracking through those places so shallowly pressurized that your limbs would explode with decompressive force if you were to "sink" down to them. These baffling, tiny men drill in toward you and your people in outlandish machines, communicating among each other in a way that you literally cannot comprehend: vocalization and phonetic writing are incomprehensibly alien to you, having adapted to thrive in a hyper-dense, universally aquatic environment.

To their eyes, you seem like a bizarre sea monster: endless, translucent chitin and tendril, sinew and scythe, a creature without bilateral symmetry or gender or a face.

But to you, these humans look like *things that cannot be.*

Their planet, they tell you, is also a water world. They have rough analogues for you and your people in the form of highly intelligent mimicking octopi and problem-solving squid and clever pack-hunting dolphins and shapeless things crowded around the black-smoke vents at the bottom of the ocean . . . but you have literally *nothing* to compare these babbling tool-master things to.

What could you and these glass-encased monkeys *possibly* say to one another—assuming you were even able to communicate?

What could you think to ask them of that unseen universe outside your own planet?

What could they even offer you or tell you or teach you?

A million or more words in their language have no meaning to you: air, water, wet, dry, sun, sky, star, ship, space, flight, rocket.

But other concepts, you know: hunger, loyalty, desire, boredom, fear . . . war.

They sing songs in their weird voices of mathematics and physics, of notions and truths that are just as true in their language as they are in yours. They claim to have listened to you and your kin from "the below that they call above" and to have swept from world to world in vast machines that move with speed beyond speed.

In time, your people and these humans might establish some comprehension, some rapport, trade, and tradition . . . and even some friendliness.

That, unfortunately, was not on the table between the Formless Magistrate and us. It did not share our mathematics . . . or anything else.

Its voice, finally, was the sound of ice breaking at the bottom of the world and all the starlight of a universe, which I had never known lurked far below me, rushing in and a drill, like the serrated, mile-wide cock of Satan, plunging into my people's holy land.

Pain exploded across my face, and the sound of a squealing dentist drill roared through my head. Vibration of my sinus cavities created sound across the not-vacuum between the farthest "Far" of the Sideways of my reality and the beginning of the Formless lands, and I couldn't hear myself screaming over it.

Cleon fell to his hands and knees beside to me, and I realized that I, too, was on all fours.

I must have said something.

The sound stopped, and then a shrill voice kicked up, reflecting from my sinus cavities. "Lo siento mucho. Yo había pensado que usted habló Mandarín en una tasa de siete puntos dos megabytes por segundo."

Cleon started talking, which I took as a good sign. "An . . . an understandable mistake, friend. It is the most common language of our world. We, however, speak English. Orally. Uh . . . hello. I am called Cleon Quiet, Secret King of Urartu."

It shrieked, causing blood to pour from my nose. "Hello! I am called He-Fucking-Who-Eats-Vampires. I find you highly attractive."

The thing was trying to be pleasant, I realized, as I noticed that hundreds of smile-like tumors and lipstick-smeared horse penises were sprouting from the thing's body on stalks or hovering disembodied in the air around it.

At that point, I realized that I could hear Cleon because his voice was also echoing through my body, like I was made of glass tuning forks.

I vomited again for good measure.

The thing bobbed, sort of at me and sort of not. "Good. I know. I am a doctor-expert on your spacetime. I like you."

I decided to take a chance. "We like you, too, buddy. We, uh . . . come in peace. We brought you some ambrosia, if you like that sort of thing."

"Fine gift! Allow me reciprocation!" Its skin changed colors suddenly from black to non-black-but-still-black. A million tiny, spinning clocks and watches began to appear all over the thing's body. Small, multicolored beach balls and rotating sundials and bars of light, filling from left to right, and buttons marked "play."

All of them turned on at once.

Several hundred simultaneous hours of bestiality pornography videos began playing over every inch of the thing's body. Mostly images of blond women having sex with German shepherds, for whatever reason.

Cleon and I both flinched.

The voice kicked up again: "Is right? These thing precious to your species, kept and treasured, traded and hoarded, yes? Many laws, hours, customs, and neural kinetics involved. Rare resource-involved gift-giving."

Cleon coughed, and I felt it in the back of my head in a perversely intimate way that no two friends should probably ever share. "That's . . . that's alright. We're not offended. Thank you."

The videos were beginning to focus on scat eating. I looked away. "Yeah, gee thanks. Look, we came to talk to you about this guy we want to kill. We were gonna see if you had any insights into that."

"Yes, and I help. Murder an important tradition. You find other, kill."

The thing twisted in on itself, and I finally recognized what it was doing with one of its "arms": it was flapping a bunch of sucker-like holes back and forth, open and closed, each like the mouth of a wooden marionette, as it spoke. It was making gestures like it was talking because it recognized that parts of the human anatomy made that same motion when we communicated. The lips didn't match the words at all, but it was a very polite effort.

That was not reassuring.

{§

Clinton J. Boomer, *known to his friends as Booms, resides in the quaint, leafy, idyllic paradise of Appleton, Wisconsin. He began writing before the time of his own recollection, dictating stories to his ever-patient mother about fire monsters and ice monsters throwing children into garbage cans. Boomer is a writer, filmmaker, and bartender. His short comedic films, D&D PHB PSAs, have over 3,500 subscribers on YouTube and have been viewed more than a million and a half times. He is—above all—a dad, a game-designer, a reader, and a recovering lifelong bachelor. His debut novel, The Hole Behind Midnight, was released in 2011 and is available from Broken Eye Books. Daniel O'Brien, columnist for Cracked.com and contributor to the New York Times bestseller You Might Be a Zombie and Other Bad News called it "Raymond Chandler meets Douglas Adams by way of a fantasy nerd's fever dream. And it's AWESOME."*

CPSIA information can be obtained
at www.ICGtesting.com
Printed in the USA
FSOW01n0404100316
17796FS

9 781940 372198